Annie Bananie

by Leah Komaiko · illustrated by Laura Cornell

SCHOLASTIC INC.

New York Toronto London Auckland Sydney

For Annie
L.K.

For my parents
L.C.

ISBN 0-590-42844-6

Text copyright © 1987 by Leah Komaiko.

Illustrations copyright © 1987 by Laura Cornell

All rights reserved. Published by Scholastic Inc.,
730 Broadway, New York, NY 10003, by arrangement with
Harper & Row, Publishers, Inc.

12 11   09 08 07 06 05 04 03 02

Printed in the U.S.A.   08

First Scholastic printing, April 1990

Annie Bananie,
My best friend,

Said we'd be friends to the end.

Made me brush my teeth with mud,
Sign my name in cockroach blood,

Tie my brother to the trees,
Made me tickle bumblebees.

Promised we would always play.

Now Annie Bananie's going away.

Annie Bananie
Wouldn't be
Annie Bananie if it weren't for me!

She was Ann
From outer space.

I scrubbed the freckles off her face.

Made her grow a half inch taller,
Shrunk her ears,
Made both feet smaller.

Brought her out for all to see—

Princess Annie Ba-nanie.

Annie Bananie,
Do you think it's good
Leaving your whole neighborhood?

Who will feed your porcupine?
Who will swing from your clothesline?

How can you just go away?
What about my sixth birthday?

Annie Bananie,
Do not cry—

Even best friends say good-by.

Make some new friends,
Try to write,

And when you are in bed at night,
Remember…

You will never ever ever

Find a friend who's half as clever.

You will never ever find
Someone who's as sweet and kind.

No you'll never

Ever ever

Never ever

Ever

Find another friend like me.